This book belongs to:

TIFFANY

ALADDIN
and other Favorite Tales

Modern Publishing
A Division of Unisystems, Inc.
New York, New York 10022
Printed in Italy

Contents

Long ago, in a kingdom very far away, there lived a young boy named Aladdin who was the son of a tailor. But Aladdin was very lazy and didn't learn his father's trade. Instead, he spent his days idly and was known as a good-for-nothing.

When Aladdin's father died, his mother did her best to care for herself and her son. Aladdin was of no help to her. They were very poor.

One day, a well-dressed man saw Aladdin running in the streets.

"Nephew!" he rejoiced. Aladdin quickly became entranced by the man. He didn't know the stranger was an evil wizard who had selected Aladdin for a wicked deed.

"Take these gold coins to your mother," said the stranger. "Tell her I wish to visit the home of my beloved brother and buy food enough for a reunion feast."

Later that night, when the sorcerer arrived, he pretended to be a long-lost relative. Aladdin's mother was suspicious but when she saw how upset he was to learn of her husband's death and how caring he was toward Aladdin, she believed him.

"I must help my poor nephew find his way in life," lied the magician. "With your permission, I will take Aladdin with me as my apprentice."

Aladdin and his mother agreed, and the next day, the two set out.

When they were far away from the city, the magician stopped walking and asked Aladdin to build a great fire. Then the sorcerer spoke magical words and threw crystals on the ground. Aladdin was startled to see the earth tremble and open up before him!

"Wear this ring and enter the caverns
below," the wizard ordered. "You will see a
lamp in a wondrous garden. Touch nothing but
the lamp or you will come to certain harm, and
bring it back to me at once."

Aladdin did as he was told, fearing the man's
wrath.

Once in the caves, Aladdin saw trees with red, green, blue and white fruit. The red fruits were rubies, the green, emeralds, the blue, sapphires and the white, diamonds. A vast treasure lay before him! Aladdin filled his pockets with as many of the pretty gems as he could carry. Realizing that no harm had come to him, Aladdin grew suspicious of his uncle. He grabbed the lamp and went back to the opening of the cave.

"Uncle, help me up," called Aladdin. "I can't make it up all the way."

"First, pass me the lamp," came the reply.

"No, uncle, it is better that I give it to you when I get out."

When Aladdin refused to hand over the lamp, the sorcerer angrily shouted another spell. The cave's entrance closed tightly. Aladdin was doomed!

"What am I going to do now?" he thought.

Forlorn and afraid, Aladdin wrung his hands together, turning the ring his uncle had given him. There was a flash and a giant appeared before him. Bewildered, Aladdin looked at the genie in fear.

"Master, command me and I will grant your wish."

"Then take me home," cried Aladdin. The genie obeyed at once.

Glad for her son's safe return, Aladdin's mother denounced the wicked man who had deceived them.

"I'll polish this lamp and sell it to buy food," she said. Before Aladdin could tell her about the jewels, Aladdin's mother rubbed the lamp. She fainted when a huge genie burst forth. "Master, command me and I will grant your wish."

"Bring us food," Aladdin commanded. In moments, the genie appeared with a golden tray set with a delicious meal.

With the power of the lamp and the riches from the caves known only to himself, Aladdin and his mother lived royally for many years.

One day, Aladdin saw the sultan's daughter
and fell in love with her. He sent his mother—
laden with the riches from the caves—to win the
sultan's approval and his daughter's love.

Never before had the sultan seen such a
wealth of jewels. His own treasury didn't possess
such a fortune. Assured that his daughter would
be happy, the sultan granted Aladdin's wish. He
and the princess were married immediately.

To show his love for the princess, Aladdin commanded the genie of the lamp to build a splendid palace as a wedding gift to her. Its magnificence was unrivaled anywhere in the world.

So great was Aladdin's wealth, that news of it travelled far and wide. The evil wizard left at once in search of the magic lamp and to ruin Aladdin.

The magician disguised himself as a merchant and tricked the princess into trading the old lamp for a shiny, new one.

Then he instructed the genie of the lamp to take the princess and the palace to a far-off land.

Aladdin called upon the genie of the ring
who took him to the sorcerer's hideaway.

Once Aladdin was reunited with his beloved princess, he destroyed the evil wizard and reclaimed the magic lamp.

The genie of the lamp returned Aladdin and the princess to their homeland. The sultan was ever so grateful for his daughter's safe return. Aladdin and the princess lived happily ever after for the rest of their lives.

One summer day, Alice and her sister were
reading in the meadow. Suddenly a White Rabbit
wearing a coat and hat ran past. He pulled out a
pocket watch and exclaimed, ''Oh dear! I'm late!''

''How curious!'' said Alice, and she ran
after him.

Alice followed the Rabbit down a rabbit hole. Along the sides of the rabbit hole were amazing things—maps, mirrors, teapots, and fruit.

"How *very* curious!" Alice exclaimed. Finally she landed—PLOP!—in a soft bed of leaves.

Alice watched the Rabbit run through a tiny
door in a hallway. "Oh dear! I'm too big to get
through the door!" she thought, bursting into
tears. Alice cried and cried until the floor was
wet with tears.

Then Alice noticed a bottle that said "DRINK ME!" And without a second thought, she did! Suddenly she began shrinking! Soon she was just the right size to fit through the tiny door.

Alice stepped through the door, and SPLASH!—she was up to her chin in saltwater. It was a pool of tears she had cried when she was so tall! "Oh dear! I don't want to drown in my own tears!" she said.

"Swim this way to shore," said a friendly Dodo bird.

Just as she dried off, the White Rabbit ran by again saying, "Oh my ears and whiskers, how late it's getting! The Queen will have my head." Then he spotted Alice. "Quick! Run home and get my gloves and fan," he told her.

The Rabbit's house was not far away. Alice
quickly found the fan and gloves—and another
little bottle. "Something interesting is bound to
happen if I drink this," she said. So she did!
BOOM! Her head hit the ceiling!

"Kill the giant!" the White Rabbit shouted. His friends began throwing rocks at Alice. Luckily, the rocks turned into tea cakes when they hit her.

"I may as well eat these," Alice thought. As soon as she swallowed one, she began to grow smaller.

Finally Alice was small enough to escape from the Rabbit's house. Wandering in the woods, she came upon a large mushroom. Sitting on it was a blue caterpillar. "Who are you?" he asked.

"I've been so many sizes today, I don't know *who* I am!" said Alice. "But I don't think I'm *my* size yet."

"Well then, I have just one thing to say," said the Caterpillar. "One side makes you taller; the other side makes you shorter."

"One side of what?" asked Alice.

"Why, the mushroom," he said.

Alice broke off a piece from each side of the mushroom. She nibbled on one side of it, then the other. First she shrank, then she grew. Her neck stretched out like a giraffe's and she banged her head against a bird's nest. "A serpent!" the bird shrieked. "Get away from my eggs!"

"Oh dear," said Alice. So she nibbled more mushroom—first one side, then the other. Finally she was just her right size. "Now what will happen?" she wondered.

"Where are you going?" said a voice. Alice turned around to see a Cheshire cat sitting in a tree.

"I don't care where I go as long as I get *somewhere*," said Alice.

"Then it doesn't matter which way you go," said the Cat. "The Hatter lives this way. And the March Hare lives that way."

At that, the Cheshire Cat began to disappear—first his tail and then his back paws. Finally all that was left was his grin. Then, that was gone, too.

"Things just get curiouser and curiouser," said Alice as she headed to the Hatter's house.

The Hatter was having tea on the lawn with the March Hare and a sleeping dormouse. When he saw Alice he shouted, "No room!"

"Why, there's plenty of room," said Alice, sitting down.

"Have some tea," said the March Hare.

Just as Alice had filled her teacup and put a cake on her plate, the Hatter shouted out, "Change places!" Everyone got up and moved down a chair. Poor Alice found herself sitting in front of an empty cup and plate.

Just then she saw a door in a tree. "Everything is so curious today, I may as well go in," she thought. And so she did.

Inside the door was a garden. Two gardeners were busy painting white roses with red paint.

"Why are you painting the roses?" asked Alice.

"We were supposed to plant a red rose bush," said one gardener. "If the Queen finds out it's . . ."

"OFF WITH THEIR HEADS!" It was the Queen.

"Never mind!" said the Queen. "Time for court!"

The Jack of Hearts was on trial for stealing the Queen's tarts. "Off with his head!" the Queen shouted.

"Not yet!" said the King. "We have not heard the witnesses."

"This is a very curious trial," mused Alice. "Oh dear, now I'm beginning to feel very curious."

"Stop crowding me," the Dormouse said
to Alice.

"I can't help it," Alice replied. "I'm growing."

"Anyone taller than a mile must leave the
court," declared the King. Everyone stared at
Alice. She tried to stand up and knocked over the
jury box.

"Off with her head!" the Queen commanded
her guards who surrounded Alice.

"I'm not afraid of you," Alice declared.
"You're just a deck of cards!" At that all the cards
rose into the air and flew around her. Alice
screamed and suddenly found herself in the
meadow again.

"Wake up, Alice," her sister said. "You've had quite a nap."

"I had the most curious dream!" Alice exclaimed. And she told her sister all about her adventures.

The Wonderful Wizard of Oz

"It's a twister," called Uncle Henry and Aunt Em to Dorothy as a cyclone hurtled toward their farmhouse in Kansas.

"Toto, Toto, where are you?" shouted Dorothy. By the time Dorothy found her little dog, Aunt Em and Uncle Henry were in the storm cellar. Outside, Dorothy and Toto faced the storm alone!

Dorothy and Toto ran into the farmhouse just as the cyclone ripped it out of the ground. Up, up the house soared into the air, twirling round and round high above the farm.

Dorothy and Toto were in the center of the terrible storm!

The house landed with a *thump* in a strange yet wonderful land. Dorothy had never seen such blue skies, colorful flowers, a brightly shining sun...or people like those walking toward her! One of them was the most beautiful woman Dorothy had ever seen.

"Welcome to Oz and the land of the Munchkins. I am Glinda, the good witch. These are the Munchkins," she said, pointing with her wand to the oddly dressed little people standing around her. "They sent for me to thank you for killing the Wicked Witch of the East."

"But I've never killed anything," said Dorothy.

"Yet there she is under your house, gone forever—except for her silver slippers which are now yours to keep," said Glinda.

"But I must get back to Kansas. Can you show me the way?" asked Dorothy.

"Only the Wizard who lives in the City of

Emerald can help you," answered Glinda. "To get there, you must follow the road of yellow bricks," she added, pointing the way.

The Munchkins and Glinda waved farewell to Dorothy, who wore the silver slippers, and to Toto, who ran eagerly ahead.

On the way to the City of Emerald, Dorothy met a scarecrow who wanted a brain so he could do his own thinking…

...and a rusted tin woodman who wanted a heart so he could have true feelings...

...and a cowardly lion who wanted the courage to become the King of Beasts.

"You all must come with me to see the Wizard," said Dorothy. "Maybe he can help you, too."

Her new friends were happy to join her. But more than anything else they wanted the Wizard to grant Dorothy's wish, so she could return home to Kansas and to Aunt Em and Uncle Henry whom she missed so very much.

On and on they walked until they came to a cliff. "What will we do now?" wondered Dorothy.

"I've got an idea," said the Scarecrow. "Tin Woodman, chop down that tree. Then we'll walk across."

"I'll go first to make sure it's safe for everyone," said the Lion, bravely.

One by one they safely reached the other side. When they did, the Tin Woodman wept with happiness—until he nearly rusted all over again!

Finally, the weary travellers reached the City of Emerald. It was so bright within the city that the gatekeeper gave each of them—even Toto— green glasses. Then they were brought to see the mighty Wizard of Oz!

"To return to Kansas…to get a brain…to
have a heart…to be courageous, you first must
destroy the Wicked Witch of the West," proclaimed
the all-knowing Wizard. Trembling, Dorothy and
her friends left the palace in search of the Wicked
Witch of the West.

Furious to learn there were strangers in her kingdom, the Wicked Witch of the West sent for her slaves, the winged monkeys. "Bring the girl to me and throw the others in the dungeon," she commanded.

Dorothy was brought before the witch. "I want those silver slippers," threatened the Witch. But Dorothy wouldn't give them up.

Unable to take the shoes, the Witch tripped
Dorothy with her cane. "You're a mean wicked old
witch," sobbed Dorothy angrily, throwing a bucket of
water on the Witch. Drenched, the witch began to
melt until she disappeared.

At last the Wicked Witch of the West was dead!
Dorothy and her friends returned to the City of
Emerald.

Soon they were standing before the mighty Wizard of Oz once again.

But when Toto pulled back a curtain in the corner of the room, they saw an ordinary man seated on a high chair working a machine that made the Wizard's face move and talk.

"Who are you?" asked Dorothy.

"I-I-I am the Wizard of Oz," he said. "Well, I'm not really a wizard," he confessed to everyone's surprise.

"You tricked us," said the Scarecrow, knowingly.

"You're a phony," said the Tin Woodman, sadly.

"What about your promises?" asked the Lion, boldly.

Although not a wizard, Oz was a wise man.

"Scarecrow, Tin Woodman, Lion," he began, "you already are smart and sensitive and brave. From this day on, you'll each have a symbol to remind you." Then he gave the Scarecrow a pincushion brain to prove he was sharp; the Tin Woodman a heart to fit into his chest of tin; and the Lion a dose of courage.

76

But the only way Oz could grant Dorothy's wish was to take her to Kansas in his balloon.

"Hurry, Dorothy," he shouted. But the balloon began to rise before Dorothy could climb in!

"How will I get home now?" Dorothy asked.

Then Glinda appeared. "Wish upon the silver slippers," she said.

Dorothy closed her eyes tightly and wished with all her heart to go back home again. Then she clicked the heels of her silver slippers three times.

In a twinkling, Dorothy was back in Kansas rushing toward Uncle Henry and Aunt Em, who were as happy to have her back as she was glad to be home again. Toto was happy to be home again, too!

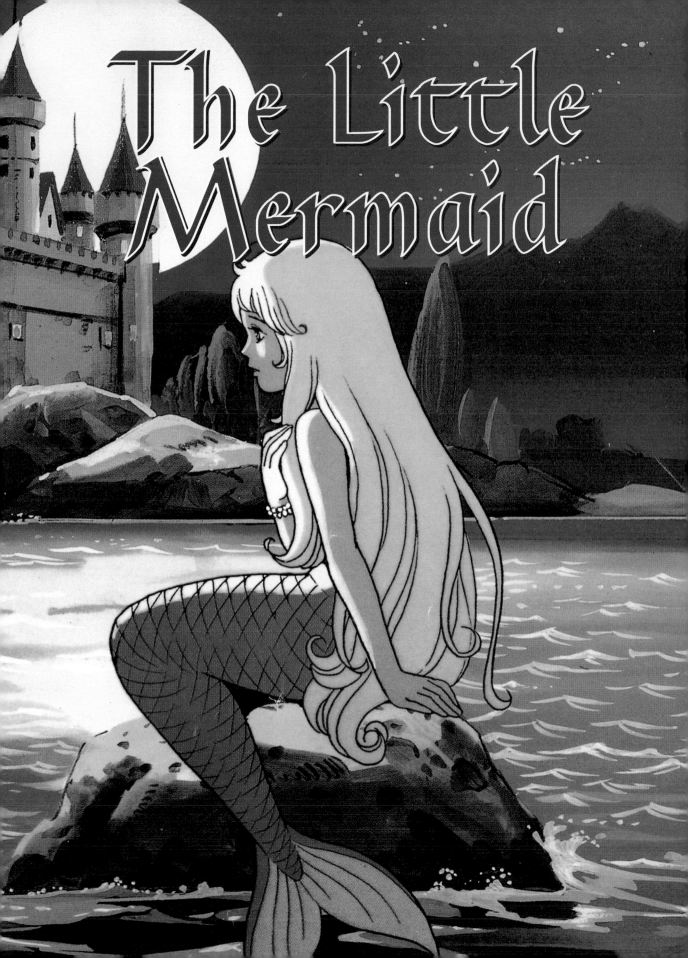

The Little Mermaid

There once was a kingdom that lay deep in the sea. The people who lived there all had tails instead of legs and could swim in the ocean like fish.

Of all the young mermaids in this kingdom, Pearlie was the youngest and kindest and she had the most beautiful voice in the sea.

Pearlie and her sisters often heard that above the water, there lived people who walked on land. People who didn't have tails, but instead had legs and feet.

Pearlie wanted so much to see this strange sight for herself, that one day, she swam up to take a look.

When Pearlie reached the ocean's surface, she saw a sailing ship. The ship's crew was shooting fireworks into the air. Bursts of colored light brightened the night sky. It was wonderful to watch.

More curious than ever, Pearlie swam closer and saw the most handsome young man she could ever have imagined. As Pearlie watched him, her heart began to flutter.

Suddenly, the lights were dimmed by black rain clouds. The night grew dark. Thunder and lightning and rough seas tossed the ship about furiously. An enormous wave crashed over the deck and the young man was swept overboard!

With a push of her powerful tail, Pearlie dove into the deep sea to save the young man from drowning.

Pearlie caught him and began swimming to shore. The storm passed quickly. Dawn was breaking when they reached the land.

"Oh, he must live," sighed Pearlie. "He is so beautiful." As she gazed down at his face, Pearlie knew she was falling in love. She then began to sing a happy song.

When the man began to wake, Pearlie slipped
back into the water and hid. A young woman
ran toward him. Pearlie watched from afar, wishing
she had legs and that he would know she had
saved him.

Pearlie followed the ship that returned the man home. She would oftentimes watch in the moonlight for a glimpse of her beloved.

When Pearlie returned to the sea kingdom, she told her sisters about the handsome man and her love for him. The mermaids knew only one person who could grant Pearlie's wish to be human — Grimalda, the evil sea hag!

Grimalda's lair was at the deepest, darkest, coldest part of the sea, where monstrous creatures and slimy serpents hid. Pearlie swam quickly.

Pearlie begged the witch to give her legs. "I will give you anything in return," promised Pearlie.

"You must give me your voice," growled Grimalda.

Pearlie trembled, but agreed to the hag's bargain. Somehow, even without a voice, she would be able to make the human understand that she loved him.

"Drink this," Grimalda ordered. She handed Pearlie a shell filled with a foul-smelling potion. After just one sip, Pearlie fell into a deep, enchanted sleep.

When Pearlie woke, she was on the beach near the castle. She had legs instead of a tail!

The young man was nearby. "Who are you?" he asked. Pearlie wanted to tell him she had saved him from drowning but she couldn't utter a word.

Taking pity on her, the young man brought her to his castle and spoke to her kindly.

Pearlie soon discovered that he was a prince and that he was soon to be married. Her eyes filled with tears and her heart broke. She would never be able to win his love and could never return to the sea kingdom.

One evening, Grimalda appeared.
"So he loves another," she crowed,
glad for the mermaid's misery.
"I'm willing to give you back your
voice and tail," taunted the evil
magician. "Just kill the prince while
he sleeps. Then you can return to
the sea."

Pearlie took the dagger and walked toward the sleeping prince. As she reached him, she silently shouted "No!" and ran off.

Blinded by tears, Pearlie fell overboard into the sea. Without her tail, Pearlie couldn't swim. She sank deeper and deeper into the darkening ocean.

All at once, the black sea was filled with sparkling light and three beautiful winged creatures appeared beside Pearlie, lifting her out of the water.

"By sparing the prince, you have earned a place with us," said one of the lovely creatures.

Pearlie's heart was filled with joy. She flew off with her new friends into the light.

Once upon a time there were three little pigs named Elmer, Hubert and Pete, who lived with their mother in the country.

One day, Mother Pig said to her sons, "You are old enough now to have your own homes, so you must build them.

"Your father built this house out of plaster, wood and stone, and it is a good house, strong against the weather and sturdy, so that no wolf will ever break into it. Build your houses as your father did his, good and strong and sturdy, and you will always be safe and well. Remember, hard work pays off!"

The eldest pig, Elmer, was lazy. He did not want to lift heavy things to build his home. So he decided to build his house out of hay.

"Surely hay is plenty good enough to protect me from rain and from little old wolves," he said. His brother was not so sure.

"It doesn't look strong enough to me," said Pete.

"I will build my house out of sticks. Sticks don't weigh that much," said Hubert, who was also lazy, "but they are stronger than hay."

Hubert was just finishing his house of sticks when Pete, the youngest brother, happened by with a load of bricks.

"What are those for?" asked Hubert.

"For my house," answered Pete.

"You don't need to work with heavy bricks to build a house. Why, a stick house is plenty strong enough against the weather and any old wolf who might come by," said Hubert.

"Maybe so," said Pete. "But I want to build the best, strongest, sturdiest house I can, and I think it should be made out of bricks. Hard work pays off!"

"Crazy pig," muttered Elmer and Hubert as they watched Pete work long into the night to finish his house. "So much work for no good reason!"

Pete didn't listen. He kept on working, and soon his brick house was finished.

The next day, the three little pigs moved into their new homes.

That night, Hubert and Pete walked Elmer home. They didn't know that a wolf was lurking nearby. Elmer bragged about his new house and how much easier his was to build than his brothers'.

"It's as strong as steel!" he bragged.

"I think my stick house is even stronger!" claimed Hubert. "I dare any wolf to try and break into my house!"

"Me, too!" cried Elmer.

"We'll see about that!" the wolf giggled to himself.

117

That night, the wolf went to Elmer's house.

"Little pig, little pig, let me in."

"Not by the hairs of my chinny-chin-chin," wailed Elmer. But the wolf huffed and puffed and blew the house down!

Elmer ran as fast as he could to Hubert's house.

No sooner had Elmer warned Hubert that the wolf was near, than a tremendous banging shook the door of Hubert's stick house.

"Let me in, little pigs, let me in," the wolf sang. Hubert and Elmer sat next to each other, shaking and trembling.

"Not by the hairs of our chinny-chin-chins," squealed the pigs.

"Then I'll huff and I'll puff and I'll blow your house in," said the wolf.

Crash! In no time, the wolf smashed his way through the walls of Hubert's house!

"Yum, yum, fresh piggy for dinner!" he cried, but Elmer and Hubert got away and ran to Pete's brick home.

"A w-w-wolf is chasing us and is going to break in here!" Elmer cried.

"This door is double-thick solid wood, with a strong bolt. He can't break it down," said Pete.

Sure enough, the wolf came banging on the door. "Let me in!"

"Not by the hairs on my chinny-chin-chin," Pete shouted.

"Then I'll huff and puff and I'll blow your house in!"

He huffed and puffed but could not get in.

"See?" Pete said to his brothers. "We are safe. I was just about to make some supper. Will you join me?" He lit a fire and put the pot on to boil.

"I am tired of your tricks, and I will get you," said the wolf. So, the wolf took a giant step backwards and ran headfirst into the door. He was sure it would crash open.

But to his disappointment, it didn't. All the wolf got for his troubles was a mighty sore head! But now, he was even more determined to get inside the house.

Then the wolf spied the
chimney. He got a ladder and placed
it against the side of the house.

"There's more than one way to
get a pig," he cried, climbing up onto
the roof. "I'll just come down the
chimney!"

"Stand back!" Pete warned his brothers as he took the cover off the boiling pot.

They listened as the wolf slid down the chimney and saw him land, with a mighty *plop!* in the pot of boiling water.

"Yyyeeeowwww!" the wolf cried.

Pete opened the front door, and the wolf ran out of the house and over the hills, far, far away.

"You can stay with me while you build your new houses," Pete told his brothers. "But this time you have to promise to work hard and build them strong and sturdy."

After that, Elmer and Hubert were never lazy again. "You've learned an important lesson!" said the pigs' mother when she heard the story. "Hard work pays off."

Elmer and Hubert nodded. "It sure does!" they agreed.

Little Red Riding Hood

Everyone in the village and woods knew Little Red Riding Hood from the red velvet cloak she always wore.

One day, Little Red Riding Hood's mother asked her to take a basket of food to Grandmother, who was very ill.

Little Red Riding Hood left at once, promising to stay on the path and go directly to Grandma's.

On the way, Little Red Riding Hood met a big, furry wolf. "Where are you going, Red Riding Hood?" he asked in a friendly voice.

"To Grandma's, she's ill."

"Is it very far?" asked the wolf.

"Not very." Red Riding Hood replied.

"Which way is it?"

"Just through the woods," she told him, pointing the way as she skipped along the path.

"Wouldn't poor, sick Grandma like a bouquet of wildflowers?" the trickster suggested.

"What a good idea!" said Red Riding Hood.
She left the path to gather an armful of flowers.

The crafty wolf ran ahead as quickly as he could to Grandma's cottage, thinking only of the fine lunch these two would make!

The wolf quietly crept up to the cottage window and peeped in. He saw Little Red Riding Hood's grandmother.

Then the wolf knocked on the door with a gentle *rap, rap, rap.*

"Who is it?" called Grandma.

"It's Little Red Riding Hood," said the wolf.

"Come in," sighed the frail old woman.

With a hop and a skip, the wolf threw open the door of the cottage. His loud entry startled Grandma.

"You're not Little Red Riding Hood," she gasped. "Who are you?"

"I'm the wolf," he snarled. And in an instant, the wolf gobbled up Grandma in one big bite.

Then he smiled and licked his lips.

143

The wolf quickly dressed in
Grandma's nightgown and cap,
then jumped into her bed. Pulling
the covers up to his snout and the
bedcap down over his eyes, he
waited for Little Red Riding Hood.

"Granny," called Little Red Riding Hood at last. The door was open so she tiptoed in so as not to wake Grandma if she were asleep.

Little Red Riding Hood set the table with the cookies and juice from her basket. Then she arranged the flowers prettily in a vase. All the while the wolf watched with beady eyes from beneath the cap.

Little Red Riding Hood crept quietly up to Grandma's bed. "Granny, such large eyes you have!"

"The better to see you with, my sweet," sighed the wolf.

"Granny, such big ears you have!"

"The better to hear you with, my sweet," whispered the wolf.

"Granny, such large hands you have!"

"The better to hold you with, my sweet," spoke the wolf plainly.

"Grandmother, such big teeth you have—"

"The better to eat you with," shouted the wolf as he pounced from the bed to gobble her up in one little bite!

"Oh, my," cried Little Red Riding Hood as she disappeared into the darkness of the wolf's belly.

Tired from his meal, the wolf climbed back into Grandma's bed for a nap.

A huntsman, passing the cottage, heard Little Red Riding Hood's cry. He quietly opened the door and saw the sleeping wolf. "At last, I've caught you, you old rascal," the huntsman said. Noticing the wolf's bulging stomach and that no one was in the house, the huntsman knew something was wrong.

He quickly snipped open the wolf and out popped Little Red Riding Hood, whose cloak was just a little bit wrinkled. A few more snips and out jumped Grandma, who stretched and complained that it was dark and cramped inside the wolf. They were both happy to be free again.

Little Red Riding Hood gathered some stones.
The huntsman filled the wolf's stomach with
them and Grandma sewed the beast back up
with a few quick stitches. The weight of the
stones killed the wolf before he could wake up
and cause more trouble.

Grandma felt much better after having some of the cake and juice Little Red Riding Hood brought in her basket. The huntsman and Little Red Riding Hood had a snack too.

Later, the huntsman walked Little Red Riding Hood home. As she waved goodbye to Grandma, Little Red Riding Hood promised never to wander into the woods alone or talk to strangers again.

And she never did.